MR.SMALL

by Roger Hargreaves

WORLD INTERNATIONAL

Mr Small was very small. Probably the smallest person you've ever seen in your whole life.

Or perhaps the smallest person you've never seen in your whole life, because he was so small you probably wouldn't see him anyway.

Mr Small was about as big as a pin, which isn't very big at all, so perhaps we should say that Mr Small was as small as a pin!

Mr Small lived in a small house underneath a daisy at the bottom of Mr Robinson's garden.

It was a very nice house, although very tiny, and it suited Mr Small very well indeed. He liked living there.

Now, this story is all about the time Mr Small decided to get a job.

The trouble was, what sort of job could Mr Small do? After all there aren't that many small jobs!

Mr Small had thought about it for a long time, but hadn't had any ideas.

Not one!

He was thinking about it now, while he was having lunch.

He was having half a pea, one crumb, and a drop of lemonade.

Mr Small thought and thought while he was eating his big lunch, but it was no use.

Thinking just made him thirsty, so he had another drop of lemonade.

"I know," he thought to himself. "After lunch I'll go and see Mr Robinson and ask his advice."

So after lunch he left his house and walked to Mr Robinson's house at the top of the garden.

It was quite a long walk for somebody as small as Mr Small, and halfway there he stopped for a rest.

He sat on a pebble feeling quite out of breath.

A worm crawled by, and stopped.

"Good afternoon, Mr Small," said the worm.

"Good afternoon, Walter," said Mr Small to the worm, whom he knew quite well.

"Out for a walk are you?" asked Walter.

"Going to see Mr Robinson," replied Mr Small.

"Oh!" said Walter.

"About a job," added Mr Small.

"Oh!" said Walter the worm again, and crawled off.

Walter was a worm of very few words.

After he'd rested for a while Mr Small set off again
and walked all of the rest of the way to
Mr Robinson's house without stopping once.

When he got there he climbed up the steps to
Mr Robinson's back door.

He knocked at the door.

Nobody heard him!

He knocked again at the door.

Nobody heard him!

The trouble was, you see, that if you're as small as
Mr Small you don't have a very loud knock.

Mr Small looked up.

There, high above his head, was a doorbell.

"How can I ring the bell when I can't reach it?" thought Mr Small to himself.

He started to climb up the wall, brick by brick, to reach the bell.

He had climbed up four bricks when he made the mistake of looking down.

"Oh dear," he said, and fell.

Bang!!

"Ouch!" said Mr Small, rubbing his head.

Just then Mr Small heard footsteps.

It was the postman.

The postman came to the door, posted his letters, and was just about to leave when he heard a voice.

"Hello," said the voice.

The postman looked down.

"Hello," he said to Mr Small. "Who are you?"

"I'm Mr Small," said Mr Small. "Will you ring the bell for me?"

"Of course I will," replied the postman in answer to Mr Small's question, and reaching out he pressed the bell with his finger.

"Thank you," said Mr Small.

"My pleasure," said the postman, and off he went.

Mr Small heard footsteps coming to the door.

The door opened.

Mr Robinson opened the door and looked out.

"That's funny," he said. "I'm sure I heard somebody ring the bell!"

He was about to shut the door when he heard a little voice.

"Hello," said the voice. "Hello, Mr Robinson."

Mr Robinson looked down, and down.

"Hello," he said. "What are you doing here?"

"I've come to ask your advice," said Mr Small to Mr Robinson.

"Well," said Mr Robinson. "You'd better come in and have a talk."

Mr Small followed Mr Robinson into the house, and, perched on the arm of Mr Robinson's favourite chair, he told him how he couldn't think of a job that he could do.

Mr Robinson sipped a cup of tea, and listened.

"So you see," Mr Small explained, "how difficult it is."

"Yes, I can see that," said Mr Robinson. "But leave it to me!"

Mr Robinson knew a lot of people.

Mr Robinson knew somebody who worked in a restaurant, and arranged for Mr Small to work there.

Putting mustard into mustard pots!

But Mr Small kept falling into the pots and getting covered in mustard, so he left that job.

Mr Robinson knew somebody who worked in a sweetshop, and arranged for Mr Small to work there.

Serving sweets!

But Mr Small kept falling into the sweet jars, so he left that job.

Mr Robinson knew somebody who worked in a place where they made matches, and arranged for Mr Small to work there.

Packing matches into boxes!

But Mr Small kept getting shut in the boxes with the matches, so he left that job.

Mr Robinson knew somebody who worked on a farm, and arranged for Mr Small to work there.

Sorting out the brown eggs from the white eggs!

But Mr Small kept getting trapped by the eggs, so he left that job.

"What are we going to do with you?" Mr Robinson asked Mr Small one evening.

"Don't know!" said Mr Small in a small voice.

"I've got one more idea," said Mr Robinson. "I know somebody who writes children's books. Perhaps you could work for him."

So, the following day Mr Robinson took Mr Small to meet the man who wrote children's books.

"Can I work for you?" Mr Small asked the man.

"Yes you can," replied the man. "Pass me that pencil and tell me all about the jobs you've been doing. Then I'll write a book about it. I'll call it *Mr Small*," he added.

"But children won't want to read a book all about me!" exclaimed Mr Small.

"Yes they will," replied the man. "They'll like it very much!"

And you did.

Didn't you?

3 Great Offers For Mr Men Fans

1 FREE Door Hangers and Posters

In every Mr Men and Little Miss Book like this one you will find a special token. Collect 6 and we will send you either a brilliant Mr. Men or Little Miss poster and a Mr Men or Little Miss double sided, full colour, bedroom door hanger. Apply using the coupon overleaf, enclosing six tokens and a 50p coin for your choice of two items.

Egmont World tokens can be used towards any other Egmont World / World International token scheme promotions, in early learning and story / activity books.

Posters: Tick your preferred choice of either Mr Men ☐ or Little Miss ☐

Door Hangers: Choose from: Mr. Nosey & Mr Muddle ☐, Mr Greedy & Mr Lazy ☐, Mr Tickle & Mr Grumpy ☐, Mr Slow & Mr Busy ☐ Mr Messy & Mr Quiet ☐, Mr Perfect & Mr Forgetful ☐, Little Miss Fun & Little Miss Late ☐, Little Miss Helpful & Little Miss Tidy ☐, Little Miss Busy & Little Miss Brainy ☐, Little Miss Star & Little Miss Fun ☐.
(Please tick)

2 Mr Men Library Boxes

Keep your growing collection of Mr Men and Little Miss books in these superb library boxes. With an integral carrying handle and stay-closed fastener, these full colour, plastic boxes are fantastic. They are just £5.49 each including postage. Order overleaf.

3 Join The Club

To join the fantastic Mr Men & Little Miss Club, check out the page overleaf NOW!

Join Our Club!

MR·MEN & little miss CLUB

When you become a member of the fantastic Mr Men and Little Miss Club you'll receive a personal letter from Mr Happy and Little Miss Giggles, a club badge with your name, and a superb Welcome Pack (pictured below right).

You'll also get birthday and Christmas cards from the Mr Men and Little Misses, 2 newsletters crammed with special offers, privileges and news, and a copy of the 12 page Mr Men catalogue which includes great party ideas.

If it were on sale in the shops, the Welcome Pack alone might cost around £13. But a year's membership is just £9.99 (plus 73p postage) with a 14 day money-back guarantee if you are not delighted!

HOW TO APPLY To apply for any of these three great offers, ask an adult to complete the coupon below and send it with appropriate payment and tokens (where required) to: Mr Men Offers, PO Box 7, Manchester M19 2HD. Credit card orders for Club membership ONLY by telephone, please call: 01403 242727.

To be completed by an adult

❑ **1.** Please send a poster and door hanger as selected overleaf. I enclose six tokens and a 50p coin for post (coin not required if you are also taking up 2. or 3. below).

❑ **2.** Please send __ Mr Men Library case(s) and __ Little Miss Library case(s) at £5.49 each.

❑ **3.** Please enrol the following in the Mr Men & Little Miss Club at £10.72 (inc postage)

Fan's Name:_____Fan's Address:_____

_____Post Code:_____Date of birth:___/___/___

Your Name:_____Your Address:_____

_____

Post Code:_____Name of parent or guardian (if not you):_____

Total amount due: £_____ (£5.49 per Library Case, £10.72 per Club membership)

❑ I enclose a cheque or postal order payable to Egmont World Limited.

❑ Please charge my MasterCard / Visa account.

Card number: | | | | | | | | | | | | | | | | |

Expiry Date: _____/_____   Signature: _____

Data Protection Act: If you do **not** wish to receive other family offers from us or companies we recommend, please tick this box ❑. Offer applies to UK only